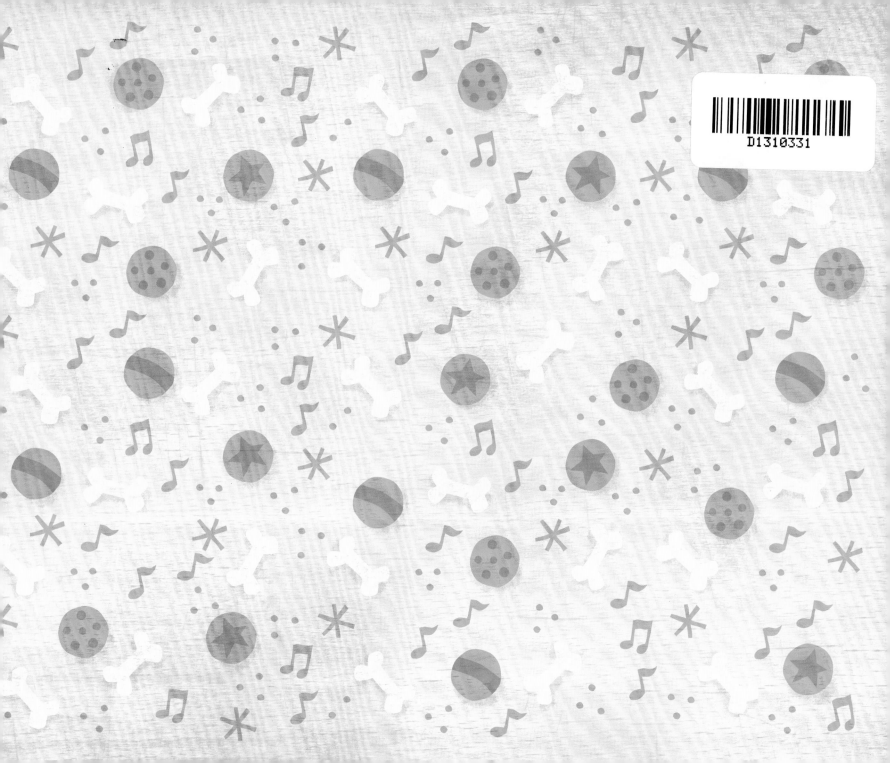

For Donny and Zooey and Oliver
my twinkle–bright stars

Title : A Tip Tap Tale
Text : Denise Gallagher
Illustrations : Denise Gallagher
ISBN: 978-1-946160-09-6
© 2017 Denise Gallagher
Printed on acid free paper in Canada

University of Louisiana at Lafayette Press
PO Box 40831
Lafayette, LA 70504
www.ulpress.org

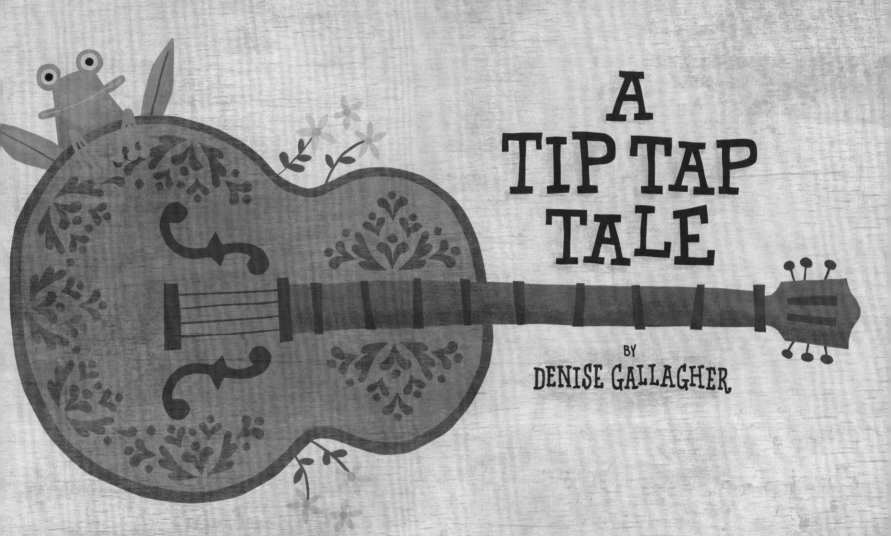

A TIP TAP TALE

BY
DENISE GALLAGHER

There is a swamp way down South
with knob-kneed trees
dripping with moss,
snow white egrets and
impossible sky-blue skies.

A dreamy-eyed dog
lives there.
A dog named BouZou—
an ears-long, tail-longer,
Louisiana mud-brown hound dog.

On moonful nights
that hound dog sings—
an eyes-shut-tight,
nose-to-the-stars,
magical, howling song.

A tip-tap tail keeps the beat.
A tune pluck-plucked
from a hand-me-down guitar.

Lightning bugs flicker
to show they approve.
Crawdads and bullfrogs,
mud-deep, hum along.

Now and again, BouZou stops,
mid-song,
to deal with a flea.
Hind leg thumping,
the fur flies.
But the crawdads and bullfrogs
keep right on humming
'til BouZou continues his song.

"I'm just a hound dog"
BouZou sings,
flashing a toothful,
canine grin at the
twinkle-bright stars above.
The crawdads and bullfrogs
and stars smile back.

One day, a silver-shining Cadillac
squished through the muck
and the mud,
Slick Jim Jack at the wheel.

Gold teeth flashing,
this cat was checking out a rumor,
a story told by Shady Sadie
about a hound dog—
a singing,
guitar-playing hound dog.

With a sly wink and a
whisker-swish, Slick Jim Jack
filled BouZou's head
with tales of New-Aw-Leens
and promises
of a glistening, gold guitar,
t-bone steaks, endless rubber balls
and a roaring, rumbling Cadillac
of his very own.

"Just come with me
and sing that song—
that crazy, rockin',
hound dog song."

The vision of his name aglow
in neon-tall
made BouZou shiver
from his tip-tap tail
to that hound dog nose.

So he packed a sack
and grabbed his guitar.

A heart-beat thump,
a slick-cat purr, and
that Cadillac squealed
as they hit the road.

First stop there in New-Aw-Leens was
Dandy Dixie's Duds,
the hippest shop for happenin' hounds.

Dixie fitted that dog up
with the absolute shiniest
sequined coat,
va-va-voom,
velvet pants with rhinestone studs
and shimmer-shiny
shoes to match.

Fancy FiFi's Beauty Shop Galore

Then off they hopped to
Fancy FiFi's Beauty Shop Galore.
Powder puffed and perfume spritzed
as that pink, perky poodle
whirled and twirled.

"A pedicure! A pompadour!"

A curl, a snip
a dab, a gab
and FiFi's work was done.

Slick Jim Jack was on the line
with the debonaire DJ,
Rockin' Jacques LaLoup...

who rang up MiMi Motormouth,
the fastest way
to spread the news.

MiMi called her best friend Spike
and she couldn't help but shout...

I've got the SKINNY on a show Tonight! a ROCKIN' HOUND! A HIP, HOT DOG! He's OUTTA SIGHT! I've Heard

And sure enough he showed them—
that jumpin' jivin' hound—
a midnight howl,
a shimmy-shake,
a tearful harmonious tune.

A triple-twist.
A turn-about.
The crowd
just couldn't get enough.

What a DOG!

You CRAZY DOG

PLEASE

Sing us one

MORE SONG!

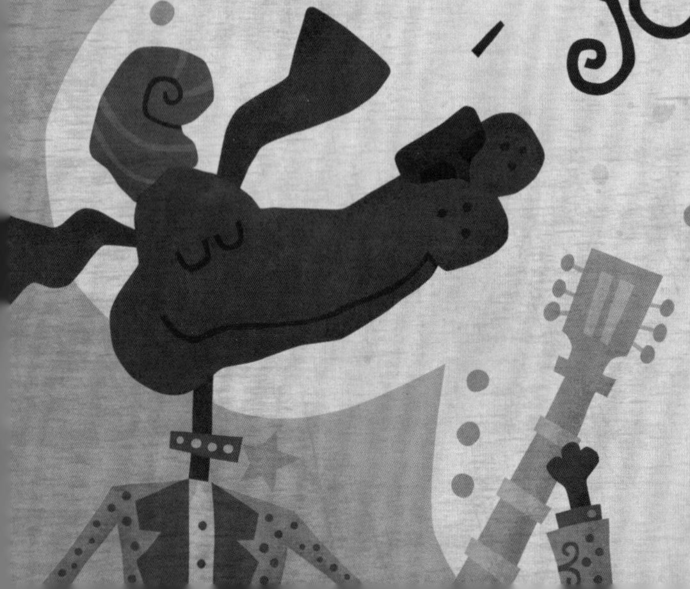

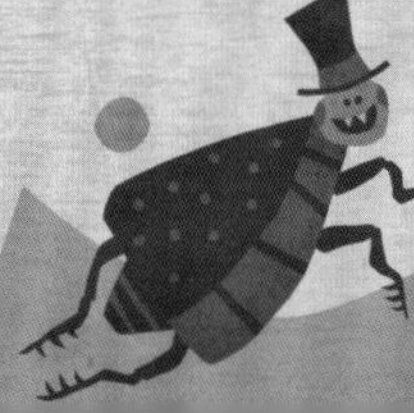

During his encore
BouZou felt an itch,
the unmistakable scratch
of a nibbling flea.
So he dropped that guitar
and his hind leg went to work.

Then he noticed the crowd
had grown silent.
"He's just an old hound dog!"
he heard in a hush.

It was enough to make a
hound dog pause,
and deep inside
he missed
the smiling stars,
the knob-kneed trees,
the lightning bugs and
bullfrogs' hum—
the place where a dog could be a dog.

So he gave a wink
and a deep bow-wow,
and be-bopped out the door.

pssst!

He headed on back,
Cadillac top down,
to the mud-brown mud
that was home.

But now and then
the full-moon glitter
calls him back,
flea powder in hand.

To howl a tune,
to jump and jive,
to twist and
hear them shout...

As a child, Denise Gallagher wrote and drew constantly. She went on to study art and graphic design at the University of Southwestern Louisiana where she earned her Bachelor of Fine Arts degree. Drawing from her rich imagination and the inspiration of her Louisiana home, she creates work that is at once whimsical and mysterious. She has illustrated books, including the Cajun folk tale *Jean le chasseur et ses chiens*, by Barry Ancelet. Denise has received awards from the Society of Illustrators New York, the Society of Illustrators Los Angeles, *Communication Arts Magazine*, and the Society of Children's Book Writers and Illustrators. Her work has been displayed in museums and galleries in New York, Los Angeles, Portland, and throughout Louisiana. She currently is happily residing in a little patch of sun in Lafayette, Louisiana, with her loving husband, two sons, and a couple of lazy hound dogs.

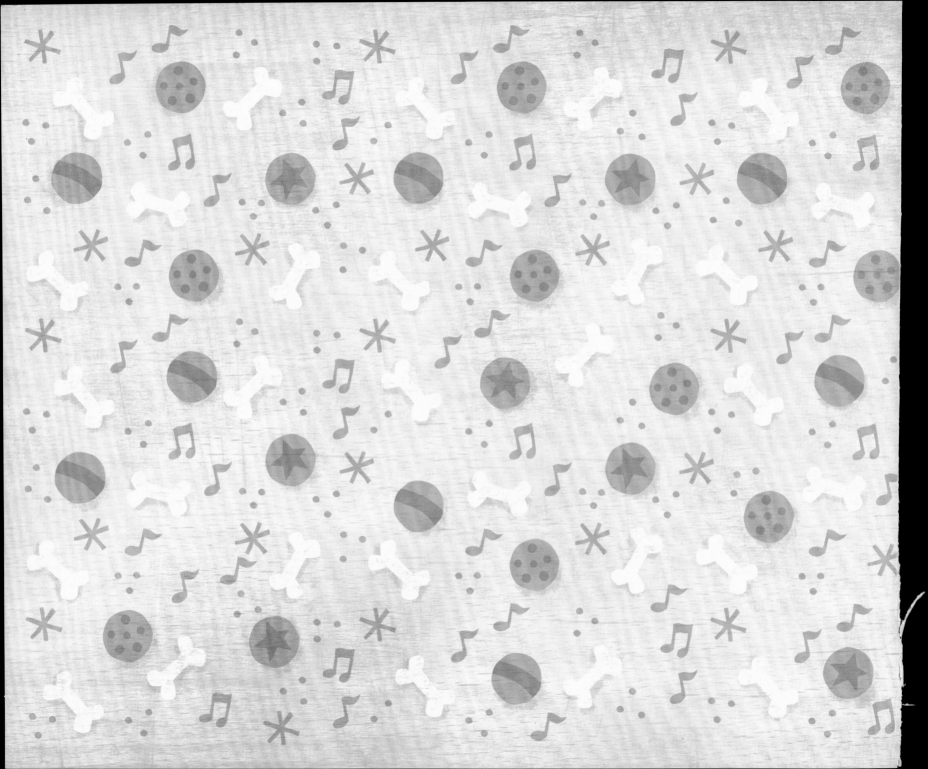